Come With Me

by Ashley Wolff

E. P. DUTTON
New York

Published in the United States by E. P. Dutton,
a division of Penguin Books USA Inc.

Published simultaneously in Canada by
Fitzhenry & Whiteside Limited, Toronto

Designer: Barbara Powderly

Printed in Hong Kong by South China Printing Co.
First Edition   10 9 8 7 6 5 4 3 2 1

Library of Congress Cataloging-in-Publication Data

Wolff, Ashley.
    Come with me / by Ashley Wolff.—1st ed.
        p.   cm.
    Summary: A little boy tells a newborn puppy all the
things they'll do in the meadow and by the sea when
the puppy is old enough to come to live with him.
    ISBN 0-525-44555-2
    [1. Dogs—Fiction.]   I. Title.   89-34482
PZ7.W8185536Co   1990   CIP
[E]—dc20   AC

for Klaus Heinrich Wolff,
in loving memory

Pumpkin,
you're just a little girl,
still too young to leave your mother.
But when it's time to bring you home,
you'll be old enough to come with me.

I'll take you
on my favorite walk,
down through
the meadow,
down to the sea.

On our way we'll stop
to scratch the red calf's chin,

and whisper good morning
to Trinity's foal.

When we get to the pond,
we'll hide in the reeds—
shhh—and see
if there are ducklings yet.

I bet the wind will tickle your ears.
Grandpa says it blows
across the Pacific, all the way from Japan.

We'll wiggle through the weeds,
and if we listen carefully,
we might hear ...

sea lions, barking
on the rocks below.

I'll race you to the waves.
You'll charge right in
and get completely soaked, then . . .

shake all over me!

You'll meet hermit crabs and starfish,

and help me find the perfect shell
I'm always looking for.

When the fog rolls in,
we'll head for home.
If you're tired, I'll carry you.
My legs are longer than yours,
you know.

On the way we'll stop for cookies. My favorite ones are chocolate-chip. I'll buy *you* some gingersnaps, and we'll have them with milk when we get home.

Oh, Pumpkin, I can hardly wait.
You'll be so glad you came.

E
Wolff, Ashley.
Come with me

DATE DUE		
JAN 3 1 1995		
		•

5/90